Down the Snake

'Down the Snake'
An original concept by Jill Atkins
© Jill Atkins

Illustrated by Izzy Evans

Published by MAVERICK ARTS PUBLISHING LTD
Studio 11, City Business Centre, 6 Brighton Road,
Horsham, West Sussex, RH13 5BB
© Maverick Arts Publishing Limited August 2021
+44 (0)1403 256941

A CIP catalogue record for this book is available at the British Library.

ISBN 978-1-84886-802-1

www.maverickbooks.co.uk

Brown

This book is rated as: Brown Band (Guided Reading)

Down the Snake

Written by Jill Atkins

Illustrated by
Izzy Evans

Chapter 1

As soon as his dad had parked the car, Kiran climbed

out and ran in through the iron park gates. He stood

staring around him in amazement.

The new park was enormous! He'd been waiting all week to come here. It was still early morning so there was no one about. They had it all to themselves!

"Look at this!" he shouted over his shoulder as his brother, Aran, and cousin, Jen, caught him up. "We're going to have a great day!"

Aran and Jen stood beside him for a moment.

"The play area looks great," said Aran.

Jen pointed into the distance. "I can't wait to climb those trees,"

she said.

"Me neither," said Aran.

"Let's explore first," said Kiran.

At that moment, Kiran's dad and Uncle Liam joined them. They all walked further into the park. They chose a spot to make a base. It was on the edge of a steep slope.

Kiran shaded his eyes as he peered down the slope.

"I wonder what's down there," he said. "There are lots of lines drawn on the ground."

"And they're all different colours," said Aran.

"Let's go and see," said Jen.

Leaving their dads sitting on the grass, they raced down the slope. When they reached the bottom, they stopped and stared.

A large flat area was covered in lines criss-crossing each other, making up a set of squares.

"This is cool," said Jen as they ran into the middle of the area. "The squares are numbered... up to one hundred."

Kiran felt a shiver of excitement. He was beginning to understand what this might be.

"Look at these squares," said Aran. "There's a ladder painted across them."

"And I can see snakes," shouted Jen.

Kiran laughed. "It's a giant Snakes and Ladders board!" he shouted. "Let's play!"

They searched for a dice and counters.

"Here's the dice," Jen called as she fetched a huge white cube from behind a bush. She brought it over for the boys to see. She turned it over and over to show them the black spots on each side.

"But we don't have any counters," said Aran.

"Yes, we do," said Kiran. "We're the counters. You're the youngest, Aran, so you can go first."

They raced to stand on square number 1. Aran took the dice from Jen and rolled it.

"Four!" he shouted and ran along to the right number.

Jen rolled a six and raced to her new square. "I'm in the lead!" she shouted.

Kiran was surprised at how light the dice was. It rolled a long way before stopping on a three.

"Aha!" he cried, running to the third square. "A ladder! Up I go!"

The ladder was quite long, and Kiran landed on square 45. They each had several turns. Aran went up a short ladder on his third go, but no one went down a snake.

Then it was Kiran's turn again. He rolled the dice.

"Five," he said. He began to step along the squares, counting as he went. "One, two, three, four, five... Oh no! A snake! Here I go!"

He ran along the snake's back.

Then suddenly, there was a loud creaking sound and the square in front of him opened up.

At the same time, the snake seemed to tilt downwards.

"Oh no!" Kiran dug in his heels and clenched his fists, but he could not stop. He slid into the hole. Down and down he sped. The slope was steep and went round in a spiral like a helter-skelter ride. He thought it would never stop!

Chapter 2

Kiran landed on his bottom with a bump. It was very dark, and he could feel his heart pounding in his chest. He was shaking all over. Where was he? And how was he going to get out?

"Help!" he shouted. His voice echoed around him. Then there was silence.

I mustn't panic, he thought.

He took some deep breaths and sat very still. Gradually, his body stopped shaking and his heartbeat slowed. Then he blinked until his eyes got used to the darkness. As he peered around, he noticed a small flame torch above his head. Its flickering light showed rough walls and a curved ceiling. He seemed to be in a large cave.

"I'll explore," he whispered. "There must be a way out."

But before he could move, he heard a shout. There was a rushing sound, a giggle and another shout. A moment later, two figures shot down the chute behind him. Aran and Jen landed in a heap.

"It's dark," whispered Aran. "I can't see."

His trembling voice told Kiran that his little brother was as scared as he was.

"Kiran, are you there?" whispered Jen.

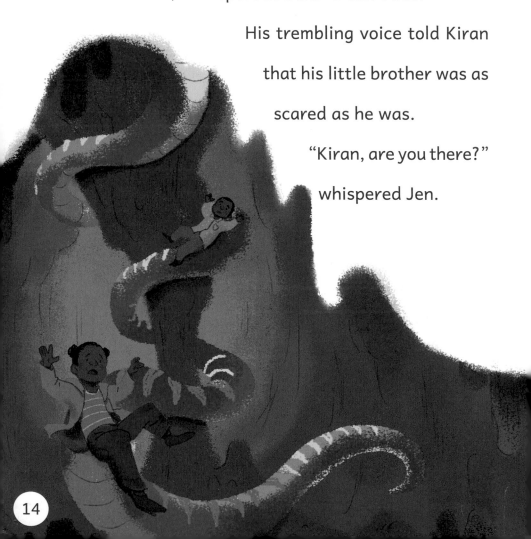

"Yes," Kiran replied. "Over here."

Jen reached out and grasped his hands. Kiran felt braver now he wasn't alone. He was the oldest. He had to take the lead.

"I think we're in a cave," he said. "We need to explore and find a way out."

"Do you think we could climb up the chute?" asked Jen.

Kiran stared up at the chute. He could just see a hint of daylight, but he remembered how steep and slippery it was.

He shook his head. "There's no way we can climb up there."

They stayed close together as they stood up. Jen took the flaming torch from the wall.

"This will help us," she said.

They crept slowly around the cave, feeling the rough rock walls.

"There must be a gap somewhere," whispered Kiran.

But the walls seemed strong all the way round. There was no way out!

Suddenly, they all froze on the spot. Kiran tensed. He had heard a faint hissing sound in the silence.

"What was that?" whispered Jen.

They listened, holding each other's hands. The hissing came from behind them. It was louder the second time, as if it were coming nearer.

Jen swung the torch round.

"A snake!" she yelled.

Kiran turned. A long snake was slithering slowly towards them from the darkest corner of the cave. Terrified, they began to back away from it. Kiran shuddered. He wondered if the snake was venomous. He had to think of a way to escape from it.

At that moment, he tripped and put his hand on a rock to steady himself. He felt something long and smooth. He whipped his hand away, thinking it might be another snake. But then he thought about it. Snakes are scaly. This was not a snake. He picked it up.

"Look at this!" he whispered.

Jen and Aran stared.

"A pipe," gasped Jen.

"It's a bit like a recorder," said Aran.

Kiran nodded. He had learned to play the recorder at school.

"I wonder..." he whispered as an idea began in his brain.

"I saw a film once," whispered Jen. "A man charmed a snake..."

"Exactly!" said Kiran. "It's worth a try."

The snake's tongue flickered like the torch flame. Kiran put the instrument to his lips and began to play a simple tune he had learned by heart. The snake stopped and seemed to be listening. Then it lifted its head and half of its body off the ground and began to sway.

"It's working!" whispered Jen. "It's dancing to the music!"

"What do we do now?" asked Aran.

As if in answer to Aran's question, there was a loud grinding sound and part of the cave wall began to slide. A narrow gap appeared. Kiran could see a light beyond the gap. He kept playing and the snake kept dancing while they slowly moved sideways towards the gap. At last, Kiran stopped blowing and dropped the pipe.

"Run!" he shouted.

Chapter 3

As the children rushed out of the cave, the gap in the wall slid shut.

They were in a long passage, which was lit by a line of green, blue and red lights. Kiran heaved a huge sigh of relief. That snake was rather scary!

"I'm glad we got out of there," he said.

"Yeah," said Aran. "Though I wasn't scared at all."

Kiran laughed. His brother had to be kidding!

"Come on," he said. "Let's see if this passage leads us to the exit."

"There's a really bright light ahead," said Jen as she raced in front of the boys. "Maybe it's sunlight."

She stopped as she reached a doorway. Turning, she shook her head.

"It's just another cave," she said.

Kiran tried to hide his disappointment as he caught up with Jen. He shaded his eyes as he peered into the cave. It was so brightly lit. The walls and the floor were smooth and clean, and the ceiling was a high arch.

"Look!" exclaimed Aran as he rushed into the cave "Here's a throne!"

The throne was right in the centre of the room. It was tall and narrow and covered in jewels. There was a red cushion on the seat.

"It's amazing!" said Jen.

"I'm going to sit on it!" shouted Aran.

Kiran felt a shiver run down his spine.

"I'm not sure..." he began, but Aran had already climbed up and was sitting proudly on the cushion.

"It's great up here," he called. "Why don't you try it, Jen?"

He slid down and made way for Jen. She laughed as she sat there and waved her hand like a queen.

"Now your turn, Kiran," she said, jumping down.

Kiran held back. He had a strange feeling that made his stomach flutter.

"Alright," he said. "Just for a minute."

The cushion was soft and very comfortable.

Kiran smiled. He wondered what he had been worried about.

Then suddenly, he heard a sound. He whipped round as a woman appeared as if from nowhere. She was very tall with a flowing robe, long black hair and flashing eyes.

"Ha!" shouted the woman. "So you thought you would play around on *my* throne?"

Kiran slid to the floor.

"We didn't know," he whispered. "We were trying to find a way out."

"I am the great Queen Cassandra!" shouted the woman. "You have used my throne without asking. So now you must pay."

"But we have no money," said Jen.

"I don't mean money," said Queen Cassandra. "You will each have to perform a task before I will let you go."

Kiran stood between Aran and Jen, and linked arms with them. They were both trembling again. He had to show that he was looking after them.

"You!" Queen Cassandra pointed at Aran. "Here is your task." She pulled a box from under the throne.

"It's a jigsaw puzzle," said Jen.

"Yes, but all the pieces are the same colour," said Queen Cassandra.

Aran took the box and sat down. Queen Cassandra pulled out another box and thrust it at Jen. Jen opened it. Inside were hundreds of buttons.

"Sort these buttons into colours and sizes," said Queen Cassandra.

Jen was about to argue, but Kiran nudged her. She frowned, but sat down beside Aran and began to sort the buttons.

"And you," Queen Cassandra said, pointing at Kiran. "You can untangle this string."

Kiran looked at the massive ball of tangled string. It would take him hours, but he nodded and took it from her. He sat down with the others and began to unpick the knots.

Queen Cassandra went to sit on her throne.

"When you have finished," she said, "you can start all over again."

Kiran gasped. Jen was staring up at Queen Cassandra and Aran looked as if he might cry.

"Carry on!" said Queen Cassandra.

After a while, Kiran's fingers began to ache and he was worried that they would never escape.

"Aran," he whispered. "Will you sing for us? It might cheer us all up. You've got such a lovely voice..."

So Aran began to sing and Kiran relaxed a little. But all of a sudden, he was startled by a loud snore. He looked up at Queen Cassandra. She had fallen asleep!

As the queen snored, he noticed one cave wall sliding upwards.

"Keep singing," he whispered to Aran.

Slowly, he stood up and crept towards the wall.

Aran and Jen followed.

As they ducked under the wall, Aran stopped singing and the wall dropped back in place.

"Come on," said Kiran. "Let's get away from here before Queen Cassandra wakes up."

Chapter 4

Kiran led the way. They clambered over piles of rocks in a dark passage until they reached another cave. Kiran had to bend down because the ceiling was so low, but he gasped at what he saw. Spotlights shone on the walls and ceiling, which were covered in shells of all shapes and sizes.

"Here's a conch shell," said Jen. "Look how pink and smooth the inside is."

"I've found a clam shell," said Aran. "And a razor shell."

Kiran opened his mouth to tell the others about a lovely green shell he had found when...

SLAM!

A heavy metal door clanged shut behind them. Kiran looked all around. There was no other way out. They banged on the door with their fists until they were sore.

"Help!" shouted Aran.

"Let us out!" shouted Jen.

But no one came.

"What do we do now?" asked Aran. "This is the third cave we've been in and we still haven't found our way out."

Even though Kiran felt just as helpless, he was determined not to show Aran and Jen.

"But we're having a great adventure," he said.

"And we've managed to find our way out of the other two caves, haven't we?"

"But I'm tired," said Aran. "I want to go back to our dads now."

"Well, we can't," said Jen. "Unless we work out how to get out of here." She went back to the conch shell and blew into it. It made a faint shushing sound, but nothing happened. She shook her head. "It was worth a try."

Kiran wished he hadn't left the musical pipe in the first cave.

"You could try singing," he suggested to Aran. "That worked last time."

Aran sighed, then he began to sing the same songs he had sung before. But nobody fell asleep and none of the walls moved.

"I've got another idea," said Jen. "Sometimes in stories, people find a knob at the side of an old fireplace. They turn it and it opens a door into a secret passage."

"But there isn't a fireplace," Aran huffed.

"That's true," said Kiran. "But maybe one of the shells could be the answer."

"Exactly," replied Jen.

"Great idea, Jen," said Kiran. "Let's start with the biggest shells."

They rushed up and down, looking for large shells, then brightly coloured ones, then interesting shapes. They pushed them, pulled them and twisted them all, but none of the shells moved. No secret door opened.

"It's not working," sighed Aran.

Kiran stared at the shells until his eyes hurt.

He was thinking. They had tried all of the best shells. There must be an answer somewhere.

"I know!" he said. "It doesn't have to be a special one that works. Let's try the smaller ones too."

"But there are hundreds!" complained Aran.

They went around the cave again, poking and turning and tugging at lots of little shells. Kiran's fingers ached and he was beginning to think they would never get out.

Suddenly, he spotted something.

"This one looks different!" he called. "It looks like an ordinary garden snail shell."

He reached forward and twisted it.

Clunk!

A trapdoor opened up in the middle of the floor.

"Yes!" Kiran punched the air.

Carefully, he stepped forward and peered into the dark hole. There were stairs leading downwards. He turned to Aran and Jen.

"Let's go!" he said with a smile.

Chapter 5

As they ran down the steep stone steps, Kiran heard the trapdoor close with another clunk. There were a few lanterns along the way and their footsteps echoed as they hurried along. They turned left then right and soon arrived at the bottom of a flight of stairs. Up they climbed. At the top, they reached a stone wall taller than Kiran.

"Oh no!" sighed Aran. "We can't go anywhere now."

But Jen had disappeared through a gap in the wall.

"Wait for us, Jen!" called Kiran. "We need to stick together."

But when he went through the gap, with Aran right behind him, there was no sign of her. It was just another wall.

"Jen!" called Aran. "Where are you?"

Jen came around a corner. She was grinning.

"Here I am," she answered. "We're in a maze. Mazes are usually made of hedges, but this one is

made of stone. I love mazes, but this looks like a tricky one."

Kiran felt the wall and found a small ledge. Putting his foot on the ledge, he pulled himself up so he was looking over the top of the wall.

"I can see the centre of the maze," he shouted. "And guess what? There's a ladder! If we came down a snake then going up a ladder must be the way out!"

After many twists and turns and dead-ends, they were almost ready to give up when, at last, they burst into an open space. They had found their way to the middle of the maze! And there was the ladder.

"I'll go first," said Kiran. He put his foot on the bottom rung and began to climb. As he went up, the light grew brighter and he felt the warmth of the sun. Then, all at once, his head popped up above the ground. As he climbed out of the hole, he realised he was back on the Snakes and Ladders board.

"We made it!" he shouted as Aran and Jen joined him.

"Let's go and tell our dads all about it," said Jen. They raced up the hill.

"We've had a great adventure!" shouted Aran as soon as they reached his dad and Uncle Liam. "We played on a giant Snakes and Ladders board and we went underground..."

"Yeah!" interrupted Jen. "Kiran slid down a snake and we followed him. And we saw a real snake and a strange woman called Queen Cassandra..."

"And a cave full of shells," said Kiran. "And we had to escape from a maze and climb a ladder to get out."

His dad laughed. "Well that's a tall story," he said.

"Snakes... strange woman... shells?" laughed Uncle Liam.

"We can prove it," said Kiran. "Look."

He led them all back down the slope.

But when they reached the flat area at the bottom he stopped and stared. The Snakes and Ladders board and the giant dice had disappeared!

Kiran, Aran and Jen gaped at each other in amazement. How could the game have just disappeared? Then they all broke into a grin. Clearly, the park was a lot more exciting than they thought!

Discussion Points

1. How did Kiran enter the cave-like tunnels at the beginning of the story?

2. What made the jigsaw puzzle Aran had to do for the Queen Cassandra difficult?

a) All the pieces were the same colour

b) None of the pieces fit together

c) He had to do it upside down

3. What was your favourite part of the story?

4. Who found the snail shell in the cave of shells?

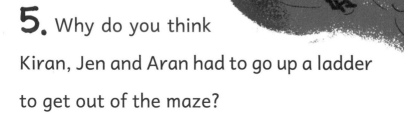

5. Why do you think Kiran, Jen and Aran had to go up a ladder to get out of the maze?

6. Who was your favourite character and why?

7. There were moments in the story when Kiran had to **solve problems**. Where do you think the story shows this most?

8. What do you think happens after the end of the story?

Book Bands for Guided Reading

The Institute of Education book banding system is a scale of colours that reflects the various levels of reading difficulty. The bands are assigned by taking into account the content, the language style, the layout and phonics. Word, phrase and sentence level work is also taken into consideration.

The Maverick Readers Scheme is a bright, attractive range of books covering the pink to grey bands. All of these books have been book banded for guided reading to the industry standard and edited by a leading educational consultant.

To view the whole Maverick Readers scheme, visit our website at

www.maverickearlyreaders.com

Or scan the QR code to view our scheme instantly!

Pink
Red
Yellow
Blue
Green
Orange
Turquoise
Purple
Gold
White
Lime
Brown
Grey

Maverick Chapter Readers
(From Lime to Grey Band)